The Pirate Musical!

Buccaneer's Edition

by Michael Tester

Baker's Plays
7611 Sunset Blvd.
Los Angeles, CA 90042
BAKERSPLAYS.COM

The original version of *THE PIRATE MUSICAL!* premiered on July 30, 2005 in a CM Performing Arts Production, with the following cast*:

AQUA MARIE, et. al . . . . Simone Catalano
BARNACLE JILL, et. al . . . . .Victoria Kaplan
BUBBA THE PIRATE. . . . . .Andrew Sklar
CAPT. KING, et. al . . . . .Timothy J. Conway
HOAGY . . . . .Dennis Carter Jr.
JACK DUSTY, et. al . . . . Rose Champion
THE MARY JANE TRAPPER, et. al . . . . Candice Cain
SABERTOOTH, et. al . . . . .Jenn Hocker
SALMAGUNDI, et. al. . . . . .Matthew Quinn
SCURVY JO, et. al . . . . .Alexander Salnikov
SHIRLEY . . . . Ashley Straw
TOMMY PIPES, et. al . . . . Michael Milan

(* Original New York workshop: Michael Devito. Susan Jeffares. Lisa Ann Goldsmith. Mickey Lambert. Doug Lilli. Matthew Senese. Pegg Winter)

CHARACTERS
(In Order of Appearance)

Note: most roles can be played by either male or female actors.

THE HEROES

NARRATOR: Can double as Baby Monkey

SHIRLEY: An imagination explorer

HOAGY: Shirley's best friend and fellow adventurer.

AQUA MARIE: The Big Mermaid

If extras are desired, they can fall into the following groups:

THE PRIMATES

CHARLIE BALANAS: The acrobatic monkey

MONKS: The surfer monkey.

ORANGUTAN RAINEE: The wise old Ape.

BABY MONKEY: The smart mouthed monkey

THE FEATHERED FRIENDS

THE THREE FLAMINGOS: Pink feathered dancers

THE COOL CATS

RITA THE CHEETAH: The Caribbean Social Director.

THE ROCK & ROLL LEOPARD: The leader of the hair-band

TINA THE TIGER: A feline Tina Turner

THE PIRATES

BARNACLE JILL: The Fleet's myopic, eye-patched navigator.

BUBBA' THE PIRATE: A.k.a. "Jolly Dodger," the French jester who dreams of being a stand-up comic.

CAPT. KING: Self-proclaimed pirate leader, intent on plundering more fame and fortune than his rival, pirate producer Long John Gold. Speaks with a British, French or Latin accent.

JACK DUSTY: Ye Ole Keeper of The Piratical Articles

THE MARY JANE TRAPPER: First Mate control freak.

TWINKLE TOES THE PIRATE: Mary Jane's personal assistant.

THE PIRATE DIVAS:

> **PIRATE PEARL:** Fashion Designer of the Nautical Stars

> **PIRATE RUBY:** The Caribbean's Next Top Pirate

> **PIRATE JADE:** Aka Hairdresser to the Spanish "Mane"

TOMMY PIPES/TAMMY PIPES: The Piratical Rapper.

SABERTOOTH and **CRUSHER:** The Pirate Guards: a single toothed swordfighter and a tattooed world wrestler

SALMAGUNDI: The Italian galley master who uses a rolling pin for a sword.

SCURVY JO: The Ukrainian bug collector

MCCAW: The Bird Watcher: Also voices the parrot on his shoulder, Polly Pepper (can be a puppet)

PIRATE MIRAGE: The Magician

SCENE & SONGS

ACT ONE

PROLOGUE:

Song 01: PIRATE PRELUDE . . . . *Shirley*

Song 02: OH MOON OF MAGIC! . . . . *Company*

SCENE ONE: THE ISLAND OF WACKY TACKY BOO

Song 03: WACKY TACKY BOO! . . . . *The Endangered Species*

   *Incidental # I: FANFARE**

   *Incidental #II MERMAID THEME** . . . . *The Pirate Band*

Song 04: ATTACK OF THE POLLUTION PIRATES! . . . . *The Pirates*

   *Incidental # III: YE OLDE PIRATE CHASE** . . . . *The Pirate Band*

SCENE TWO: THE PIRATES LAIR

Song 05: THE BIG OLE MERMAID BLUES *Aqua Marie*

Song 06: WHOEVER YOU ARE . . . . *Aqua, Shirley*

                                                   And animals

*(*These three INCIDENTAL THEMES may be repeated as needed throughout the show)*

ACT TWO

SCENE ONE: THE WACKY TACKY IDOL COMPETITION

Song 07: MONKEY SEE / MONKEY DO . . . . *The Primates*

Song 08: MONKEY BEACH . . . . *The Cool Cats*

   Ode To J-Dust . . . . *Sal, Jack, Jill, Twinkle*

Song 09: THE SCURVY LITTLE DITTY . . . . *Scurvy Jo*

   Pirate Pearl's Fashion Show . . . . *The Pirate Divas*

Song 10: PIRATE & PARROTS . . . . *McCaw and Friends*

Song 11: THE BALLAD OF MARY JANE . . . . *The Back Fleet Pirates*

   Bubba's Big Break

   Mirage's Grand Illusion . . . . *Mirage and Beautiful Assistant*

Song 12: THE PIRATICAL TAP . . . . *Mary and Twinkle Toes*

Song 13: THE PIRATICAL RAP . . . . *Tommy Pipes & Crew*

Song 14: SHAKE THAT FIN! . . . . *Shirley & her Feathered Friends*

EPILOGUE

Song 15: BONGO IN THE CONGO! . . . . *Company*

BOWS / EXIT MUSIC . . . . *The Pirate Band & Co.*

A PIRATE MUSICAL JOURNEY

I was thirteen and dressed as a pirate for Halloween when I was told by a neighbor I was too old to trick-or-treat. As she closed the door on my childhood, little did I know that decades later I would fulfill my swashbuckling fantasies by being cast adrift in the national tour of Broadway's *Peter Pan* and eventually create my own musical that would afford young explorers to shipwreck into their imaginations.

After its initial workshop *The Pirate Musical!* made its debut in 2005 at New York's CM Performing Arts Center, with *NY NEWSDAY* praising its "infectious pop score." In 2007, the musical was licensed by Baker's Plays, a subsidiary of Samuel French.

In 2009, an expanded junior version of *The Pirate Musical!* was produced by West Side Theater Association, Cold Spring Harbor, NY under the musical direction of Dr. Kenneth Gold, with choreography by Nicole Jaworowski.

We now proudly present this new version of *The Pirate Musical!,* our "Buccaneer Edition," which opens the adventure of imagination to a larger audience.

Anchors Aweigh!

Michael Tester
BroadwayClubhouse.com

ACT ONE

Prologue

*(**PRESET**: A treasure chest sits center stage, in front of a closed curtain. Garbage strewn about the stage.)*

*(**AT RISE**: A narrator opens the treasure chest and discovers a dusty old book.)*

SONG #01: 'PIRATE PRELUDE'

NARRATOR. *(reading from the book)* "Once upon a blue moon, there lived a girl who dreamed she led two lives:

SHIRLEY.

I WISH I WERE A PIRATE, I'D SAIL THE SEVEN SEAS
BEYOND IMAGINATION, UPON AN OCEAN BREEZE
SINGING SONGS OF TREASURE, I'D A'SURF A CRAZY CURL
IF I WERE A PIRATE GIRL

NARRATOR. One: that of a mild mannered student, the other; a piratical rock star! Like Hannah Montana. Only her name was Shirley. Which doesn't rhyme with Montana, or *(name of school district)*, where she lived, next door to her best friend Hoagy.

*(**HOAGY** makes a dramatic entrance.)*

He too had an alter-ego, that of explorer Indiana Hoagy! Only he was not from Indiana, but *(name of school district)* –

*(**SHIRLEY & HOAGY** pick up litter from the stage and put it into their backpacks.)*

Where Shirley and Hoagy spent their weekends clearing the stage of litter…and once in a blue moon shipwrecked into their imaginations, for the adventure, of their lives!

(Segue into SONG #02: "OH MOON OF MAGIC")

HOAGY. Can you believe at all this pollution? Candy wrappers, bottles…

SHIRLEY. Wait! Hoagy. Don't throw that out!

HOAGY. I was gonna recycle it.

*(tosses the bottle to **SHIRLEY** then exits)*

SHIRLEY. No. I mean, yes of course but, look inside…it's a message in a bottle!

(reads the message)

"Calling all Ye Imagination Explorers: If you can sing, dance, or act, you are invited to enter the Wacky Tacky Idol Competition? To be held when the moon is blue, on the magical island…of Wacky Tacky Boo." Hoagy!

(puts the message in her backpack and pulls out a life-preserver)

WHY WAIT AROUND FOR YOUR SHIP TO COME IN?
IMAGINATION'S OUT THERE FRIEND
(IT'S) TIME TO DIVE RIGHT IN!
OH MOON OF MAGIC AFAR
MAKE ME A WACKY TACKY STAR
STAND BACK, YOU'RE LOOKING AT
YOU'RE NEXT WACKY TACKY IDOL!

*(She "dives" into the ocean audience as the curtain opens to reveal the full **COMPANY** of pirates and animals in tableau. Tech Cue: Fog.)*

COMPANY.

WHO WILL LEAD OUR REVOLUTION?
WHO KNOWS WHAT TO DO?
COME CLEAN WITH A NEW POLLUTION SOLUTION?
LOOK, THE MOON IS BLUE!
RECYCLE OUR FAITH AND WE'LL BE SMILING
ONLY YOU CAN SAVE OUR GROOVY DISAPPEARING ISLAND

OH MOON OF MAGIC AFAR
SEND US A WACKY TACKY STAR!
WHOEVER YOU ARE, WE'LL BE WAITING HERE FOR
YOU!

(All point towards **SHIRLEY**, *then burst from their tableau in a mix of animal and pirate sounds and movement: the* **PIRATES** *exit in character, while the* **ANIMALS** *race towards* **SHIRLEY**. *Segue in to* **SONG #03: 'WACKY TACKY BOO')***

Scene One

(*SETTING: Monkey Beach, on the mythical shores of Wacky Tacky Boo.*)

(*AT RISE: Endangered species gather to welcome Shirley.*)

ANIMALS.

WELCOME TO THE ISLAND OF WACKY TACKY BOO
BEACHED ON MONKEY BEACH WE'VE COME TO RESCUE YOU
    CAN –
RECUPERATE YOUR BOO-BOO, WITHIN OUR CAGE-LESS ZOO
    DO –
REST YOUR FUR AND FEATHERS ON WACKY TACKY BOO
COME REST YOUR FUR AND FEATHERS, ON WACKY TACKY
    BOO!

HELLO! GLAD TO MEET YOU
ENDANGERED SPECIES ARE HERE TO GREET
YOU-CAN PLAY ON OUR JUNGLE-GYM MONKEY BARS

SHIRLEY.

OOH

ANIMALS.

COME CLIMB NATURE'S LADDER TO A COCONUT TREE!
SPLIT A BANANA WITH A CHIMPANZEE
HANG TEN ON MONKEY BEACH
MONKEY SEE, MONKEY –

CHARLIE BALANAS.

DUDE!

ANIMALS.

MAKE A FRIEND ON THE ISLAND OF WACKY TACKY BOO
CONGRATULATIONS WE LOVE YOU!

RITA THE CHEETAH. (*offering flowered garland*) Welcome To
The Island Of Wacky Tacky Boo!

ANIMALS.

FEEL FREE-TO DO WHATEVER YOU PLEASE
BUT PLEASE, OH NO, DON'T UPSET THE VOLCANO
ON WACKY TACKY BOO

SHIRLEY. There must be some mistake; I would love to help
out but...

FEATHERED FRIENDS. *(balancing on one leg)* Do a little dance,

PRIMATES. Shake the sand from your pants –

ANIMALS.

AND FOLLOW YOU TOUR GUIDE ORANGUTAN
HE GONNA' SHOW YOU THE RIVER WHERE TARZAN SWAM!
SING IN THE SHOWER OF A POWERFUL WATERFALL

COOL CATS.

SCRATCH THE TRUTH ONLY NATURES TEACHES

PRIMATES.

DINE ON THE FRUITS OF NETHER REACHES

ANIMALS.

VISIT CAVES AND COVES AND OTHER KEEN FEATURES
MAKE JEWELRY OUT OF SHELLS FROM OUR PRISTINE
    BEACHES
CONGRATULATIONS WE LOVE YOU!
WELCOME TO THE ISLAND OF WACKY TACKY BOO, FEEL
    FREE –
TO DO WHATEVER YOU PLEASE
BUT PLEASE, OH NO, DON'T UPSET THE VOLCANO
ON WACKY TACKY BOO

SHIRLEY. So um like, what happens if you upset the –?

(**ANIMALS** *scatter, screeching.*)

ANIMAL SOLOIST.

OCEANS AGO WITH A HURRICANE BLOW
POLLUTION PIRATES BEACHED THEIR BOAT
ON THE VOLCANIC SIDE OF THE ISLAND
PLUNDERIN' (AND) GARBAGE PILING!

FEATHERED FRIENDS.

BUILDING SOMETHING MYSTERIOUS

SHIRLEY.

OOH...

ANIMALS.

CHOPPING DOWN TREES DEAR TO US

BABY MONKEY.

THESE PIRATES ARE A JINX

RITA THE CHEETAH.

DON'TCHA' KNOW, WHENEVER THEY UPSET THE VOLCANO,
Child!

THE WHOLE BLOOMIN' ISLAND STARTS TO SHRINK!

SHIRLEY.

THAT STINKS

BABY MONKEY. But hey,

ANIMALS.

CONGRATULATIONS WE LOVE YOU! WON'T YOU
Help Us Save The Island of Wacky Tacky Bo?!

SHIRLEY. I knew there was a catch.

ANIMALS.

THEN YOU CAN DO WHATEVER YOU PLEASE

RITA THE CHEETAH. *(stopping* **SHIRLEY***)* Orangutan Rainee
Sing Em What The Island Harvests

ORANGUTAN RAINEE. Orangutan Means 'People of The
Forest'

PRIMATES.

WE HAVE SCARY MONKEYS, SPIDER MONKEYS,
HAIRY & BEGUILING MONKEYS
HOWLER MONKEYS, SILLY MONKEYS WEARING MONKS CAPS

FEATHERED FRIENDS.

FLOWERING PEACH BIRDS, PARROTS WHO REPEAT WORDS

COOL CATS.

CHEETAHS, STRIP-PED TIGERS, LEOPARD PRINTED COOL
CATS.

ORANGUTAN RAINEE.

AND I BELIEVE THAT'S IT FRIENDS

ANIMALS.

ANYONE WE MISSED?

FEATHERED FRIENDS.

AQUA!

RITA THE CHEETAH.

THE BIG MERMAID!

ANIMALS.
> IS NOT YOUR AVERAGE FISH
> CONGRATULATIONS WE NEED YOU TO –
> HELP US SAVE THE ISLAND OF WACKY TACKY BOO
> THEN YOU CAN DO WHATEVER YOU PLEASE
> BUT PLEASE, OH NO, DON'T UPSET THE VOLCANO

SHIRLEY.
> OH NO, NO WAY WE WOULD EVER UPSET THE VOLCANO,

ALL.
> OH NO NO, NO WAY – I WOULD NEVER UPSET THE –
>
> *(Sound cueor piano tremolo: VOLCANIC RUMBLE. All try to hold ground.)*

SHIRLEY.
> OOPS.

BABY MONKEY. Looks like *someone* upset the volcano

ALL.
> ON WACKY TACKY BOO,
> **OOH!**
>
> *(All fall down on the final musical button except three* **PRIMATES** *who strike the see no/hear no/speak no evil pose. After applause,* **HOAGY** *urgently enters.)*

SHIRLEY. Hoagy? What are you doing here?!

HOAGY. I've been shipwrecked inside your imagination for I don't know how long-you tell *me!*

> *(Sound cue: VOLCANIC RUMBLE. One by one the* **ANIMALS** *exit.)*

ORANGUTAN RAINEE. There goes another tree house –

CHARLIE BALANAS. Food!

FEATHERED FRIENDS. Protection!

SHIRLEY. *(whispers)* I didn't know flamingos were endangered.

HOAGY. Where do you think lawn ornaments come from?

RITA THE CHEETAH. Someone must stop these pollution pirates at once.

HOAGY & SHIRLEY. "*Pollution* Pirates?"

RITA THE CHEETAH. (*arms around our* **HEROES, SHIRLEY &** **HOAGY**) And *someone* has a half an hour to do so.

HOAGY. Fear not Endangered Species, Shirley's come to save the day!

(MUSIC CUE: Incidental #i)

SHIRLEY. She has?

PRIMATES. Hooray for Shirley! She's come to save the day!

RITA THE CHEETAH. Monkey see/monkey do-not just pose there; offer her a meal worm!

(SHIRLEY *is offered a gummy worm.)*

SHIRLEY. What are we on "Survivor?"

LEOPARD. We're all survivors here girl.

RITA THE CHEETAH. Now it's up to you to out-sing,

FEATHERED FRIENDS. Out-dance,

PRIMATES. And out-act,

COOL CATS. The pirates –

RITA THE CHEETAH. With Mother Nature on your tribe!

(All Ad-lib.)

SHIRLEY. But, I…

MONKS. Dude: Your natural instincts will like, totally guide you in stopping the pirates from trashing our island.

SHIRLEY & HOAGY. They will?

TIGER. Rrrrrealy.

RITA THE CHEETAH. And of course help save The Big Mermaid.

SHIRLEY & HOAGY. 'Big Mermaid?'

BABY MONKEY. In time for the show.

FEATHERED FRIENDS. 'Wacky Tacky Idol.'

RITA THE CHEETAH. That diva's been warming up her gills all season.

HOAGY. (*pulling a magnifying glass from his backpack*) Where was the last place you saw her?

MONKS. Floundering in the surf, before –

PIRATES. *(from offstage)* Timber, Timber-Shiver me Timbers!

BABY MONKEY. *(jumps on someone's back)* Pirates!

MONK. Hurry!

RITA THE CHEETAH. There's no time to lose!

HOAGY. Shirley, where's that message in a bottle we found?!

(**SHIRLEY** *retrieves the bottle from her backpack.* **MUSIC CUE: INCIDENTAL #ii.** **HOAGY** *uses his magnifying glass.*)

Just as I thought; a PS. written in fish oil:

SHIRLEY. *(reading the message)* "To Whom It May Concern: I have been captured by Pollution Pirates who are building an ark, aboard which they plan to sell poached wildlife in a floating pet shop they've christened… 'Endangered Species Are Us!?'"

(*Sound cue:* VOLCANIC RUMBLE. **END INCIDENTAL #11.** **SHIRLEY** *drops the message.*)

No wonder the volcano's upset.

PIRATES. *(throwing trash from the wings)* Timber, Timber-Shiver me Timbers!

ALL. *(others)* Pirates!

(**ANIMALS** *urgently exit.*)

BABY MONKEY. Later dudes!

SHIRLEY. Let's disguise ourselves as pirates, and infiltrate their pollution pirate pow wow!

HOAGY. Let's not.

(*They hide* **SONG #04: 'ATTACK OF THE POLLUTION PIRATES!'** **PIRATES** *navigate the Stage, building ranks.*)

PIRATES.

TIMBER, TIMBER!
SHIVER ME TIMBERS!

(*Repeat as necessary, until all* **PIRATES** *are accounted for.*)

PIRATES.

> SHIVER ME TIMBERS, SHIVER ME TIMBERS
> DELIVER ME, DELIVER ME,
> DELIVER ME TIMBER!
> **CRASH!** GOES A TREE WE'RE ON A CHOPPING SPREE
> WE ARE THE POLLUTION PIRATES.
> WE CLEAR THE CYPRESS TALL, DIG TO HEAR THE FICHUS
>   FALL.
> DEMOLITION IS OUR CALL MATEYS
> WE ARE THE POLLUTION PIRATES.
> PIRATES, PIRATES!
> NO OTHER PET DEALER IS MORE THRIFTY OR BOLDER
> HE EVEN SOLD THE PARROT OFF HIS VERY OWN SHOULDER!
>
> (WE) JUNK UP THE JUNGLE PAPER WE CRUMBLE
> WE ARE THE POLLUTION PIRATES.
> DEFORESTING THE FOREST, A MENAGERIE WE HARVEST
> THE SEAS WE DEFACE, LEAVING DRIFTWOOD ON OUR WAKE –
> SUCH

(forming a choir)

> SWEET BOTANICAL DESTRUCTION WE BRING
> WHEN WHAT WE REALLY WANT TO DO IS DANCE AND SING
> THE PLANET'S INORGANIC TYRANTS,
> TRASHING EVERYTHING, HUZZAH!
> Cross Me Skull and Crossbones!
> WE LOVE POLLUTION PIRATING!

CAPT. KING. Fabulous –

CAPT. / PIRATES.

> OLE / HUZZAH!

(SOUND CUE: PHONE SIGNAL. All break their final tableau.)

CAPT. KING. That must be Long John Gold. Fetch me my shell-phone! Wait 'till he hears of:

(Sings a capella, to the melody of music #4.)

THE BIG OLE MERMAID, we caught!

PIRATE PEARL. *(holding the conch part of a shell to her ear)* Signals bad. I can only like, hear the ocean.

CAPT. KING. *(seizes the phone)* Long John Gold's been in the market for such a –

(into the phone)

Hoy matey!

SHIRLEY. *(Offstage)* Ahoy mateys! Or something like that!

(SABERTOOTH and CRUSHER on guarde, the PIRATES scatter, as their CAPT. places his call, and a thinly disguised SHIRLEY & HOAGY enter in call-and-response cadence:)

SHIRLEY & HOAGY. We Are Pirates, That's A Fact,

PIRATES. *We* Are Pirates That's A Fact!

HOAGY. Yo Ho Ho?

SHIRLEY. Or Something Like That

PIRATES. Yo Ho Ho [Or Something Like That?]

SHIRLEY. Ahoy-vey!

(hits her head when she salutes)

PIRATES. *(returning her salute)* Ahoy-vey?

(hit themselves)

Ow.

SABERTOOTH. If ye be the factual pirates of whom ye sing then…where is thy ship?

(Other PIRATES concur.)

SHIRLEY. *My* ship?

PIRATES. *Thy* ship!

CAPT. KING. *(covering the phone receiver)* I'm on the phone!!

(back on the phone)

"Aye, Long John Gold, we've captured thee –

(Acapella to the tune of Song #05)

BIG OLE MERMAID."

BARNACLE JILL. *(looking at SHIRLEY & HOAGY thru her spyglass)* If ye be buccaneers, where is thy vessel?!

(All concur.)

SHIRLEY. We surfed?

PIRATES. Thou surfed?

HOAGY. Thou did.

CRUSHER. *(incredulous)* Part of the Olympic Surfing Team are ye?

SHIRLEY & HOAGY. Ye.

PIRATE PEARL. Then like, show us thy gold medals.

(**PIRATES** *ad lib, "Good one," etc.*)

SHIRLEY. We came in second?

PIRATE JADE. Silver, aye?!

HOAGY. No, my eyes are blue.

(*or whatever the actor's eye color*)

PIRATE RUBY. That's hot.

JACK DUSTY. If ye be sea dogs, answer this maritime riddle.

(*reads from the prologue's pirate storybook*)

'Red Sky at Morning?'

HOAGY. 'Sailor take Warning?'

TOMMY PIPES. 'Red Sky at Night?'

HOAGY. Um…'Sailor's delight!'

TOMMY PIPES. 'Red Sky during Day Light's Savings Time?'

HOAGY. You're running out of rhymes?

BUBBA THE PIRATE.. Oh this guy's good. He is *good.*

CAPT. KING. *(still on the phone)* "Have your first mate call my first mate anon."

MARY JANE TRAPPER. Me name is not 'anon!' Tis the –

CAPT. KING. 'Mary Jane Trapper' I know!

(*Continuing their inquest, the* **CREW** *confront* **SHIRLEY**.)

PIRATE PEARL. And what is thy pirate name?

SHIRLEY. My pirate name?

PIRATES. *Thy* pirate name!

PIRATE PEARL. I already know my name, duh. Tis' Pirate Pearl: Fashion consultant to the nautical stars.

(*hands* **SHIRLEY** *her card*)

PIRATE JADE. Jade: The Caribbean's Next Top Pirate.

PIRATE RUBY. Ruby: Hair Dresser to the Spanish "Mane."

MARY JANE TRAPPER. And *I* be Mary Jane Trapper. (But me stage name is, "M. Trap.")

TWINKLE TOES. And she is vice captain!

(**JACK** *and mates flips thru the book to see if this is so.*)

BARNACLE JILL. *(saluting the wrong person)* Barnacle Jill.

MCCAW. McCaw.

(**PARROT** *repeats "McCaw."*)

BUBBA THE PIRATE. Jolly Dodger – (Call me 'Bubba' and I'll sink your battle ship!)

JACK DUSTY. You've already met Tommy Pipes.

TOMMY PIPES. Yo, ho-ho, meet Private Scurvy Jo.

SCURVY JO. *(proudly)* I've got scurvy!

MIRAGE. *(coughing and blowing away dust)* Pirate Mirage: the Magical Buccaneer! Now you see me…

(waves a pirate scarf)

Now you…Still see me. It needs work I know.

JACK DUSTY. Jack Dusty 'ere. But me stage name be "J-Dust."

SABERTOOTH. Enough with the name dropping!

CRUSHER. Stop skidaddling and tell us thy pirate name!

(*His* **MATEYS** *agree.*)

SHIRLEY. 'Thy'…pirate…name? Is…Ah…Captain…

(**PIRATES** *whisper: 'Ooh she's a Captain, 'etc. ad lib.*)

Captain…

(*seeing* **HOAGY** *pick up a piece of crumbled paper that the pirates threw during Song #4*)

Clean!

HOAGY. Captain Clean?

PIRATE PEARL. That's hot.

SHIRLEY. It's been in the family forever?

PIRATES. Huzzah!

SHIRLEY. *(un-crumbles the paper to read)* "You are cordially invited to the grand opening of our floating pet shop: Endangered Species Are Us?! Free Goldfish with this coupon."

*(***PIRATES*** grab the paper and argue over who put in a coupon.)*

CAPT. KING. *(removing Barnacle's spyglass from his face)* What in Neptune be the cause of all this blunder buss?!

SABERTOOTH. These land lubbers claim to be Piratical.

JACK DUSTY. Yet they have no ship's log.

BARNACLE JILL. They have no ship.

SALAMAGUNDI. Neither ration –

THE PIRATE DIVAS. Nor fashion.

CAPT. KING. And you interrupt my call with an important client for this? Scalawags!

MARY JANE TRAPPER. *(startling the* **CAPT.***)* Scalawags!

SHIRLEY. *(whispers to* **HOAGY***)* What's a scalawag?

HOAGY. Sounds like a bug.

MARY JANE TRAPPER. *(overhears)* "Bug" did you say? Spies!

TWINKLE TOES. *(into* **MARY JANE***'s ear)* Spies!

SABERTOOTH & CRUSHER. *(en garde)* Spies!!

*(***POLLY*** the parrot echoes "Spies!")*

CAPT. KING. From a competing pet shop, I suspect? Toss these imposters into the brig with El Mermaid Mysteriouso!

*(**INCIDENTAL: #III: 'YE OLDE PIRATE CHASE.'** After a sword fight,* **SABERTOOTH & CRUSHER** *corner our* **HEROES,** *as* **MARY & TWINKLE** *throw seaweed net over them.)*

MARY JANE TRAPPER. Into the drink with the sardine!

TWINKLE TOES. Sardine!

HOAGY. Can't we just walk the plank?!

(to **SHIRLEY***)*

What? I always wanted to do that.

(LIGHT/SOUND CUE: **PIRATES** *throw our* **HEROES** *into their lair.)*

Scene Two

(SETTING: The Pirates Lair at Sun Down)

*(AT RISE: Sound cue: crickets and bullfrogs. Still beneath the netting, **SHIRLEY** borrows **HOAGY***'s *magnifying glass while hesings to himself to pass the time:)*

HOAGY. "Ninety-Nine Bottles of Water on the Wall
Ninety-Nine Bottles Water
Take One Down Pass It Around
Then Buy A Filter and Reduce Your Carbon Finger-print."
Hey. I'm a poet and I didn't even realize it.

SHIRLEY. Hoagy!

(whispers)

Is it just me, or are those fin tracks?

HOAGY. It's just you. "Ninety Eight Bottles of –"

SHIRLEY. But look, the tracks follow a trail of seaweed.

*(They remove net. **SHIRLEY** tugs on a long, seaweed boa, the other end of which is attached to the big **MERMAID**, dragging her on Stage.)*

See, it's –

(SONG #05: 'THE BIG OLE MERMAID BLUES')

AQUA MARIE.
A BIG OLE MERMAID, M.E.R.M.A.I.D.
A BIG OLE MERMAID, M.E.R.M.A.I.D.
No Autographs Please
I'M SWEETER THAN A SHARK, CUTER THAN A WHALE
A SEAWEED SIREN WITH A SAD POLLUTED TALE
A BIG OLE MERMAID, M.E.R.M.A.I.D.
A BIG OLE MERMAID

SHIRLEY.
'SWEETER THAN A SHARK?'

HOAGY.
'CUTER THAN A WHALE!'

SHIRLEY & HOAGY.

A SEAWEED SIREN WITH A SAD POLLUTED TALE

ALL.

JUST A BIG OLE MERMAID, M.E.R.M.A.I.D.

SHIRLEY.

'A BIG OLE MERMAID'

AQUA MARIE.

OH! I USE TO SWIM WITH MY KID SISTER
BEFORE SHE SWAM TO FAME

SHIRLEY.

'USE TO SWIM WITH THE LITTLE MERMAID
BEFORE SHE SWAM TO FAME?'

AQUA MARIE.

NOW WHO CAN DIVE IN THIS DIVE?
LAND LOCKED I PRAY –
ONE DAY IN OPEN WATER THESE FINS WILL SWIM AWAY

SHIRLEY & HOAGY.

A BIG OLE MERMAID, M.E.R.M.A.I.D.

AQUA MARIE.

A BIG OLE MERMAID, M.E.R.M.A.I.D.
THAT'S ME.

SHIRLEY. Excuse me, Mer-Ma'am?

HOAGY. *(referring to his field journal)* 'Aqua Marie.'

SHIRLEY. You'd better get back in the water before you dry up. No offense.

AQUA MARIE. None taken. When the moon is blue, mer-maids sprout legs and put on a show.

HOAGY. I did not know that.

(writes in his journal)

AQUA MARIE. Now if I could just clean up my act, I could get to my gig.

SHIRLEY. Wacky Tacky Idol?!

AQUA MARIE. Are you a contestant?

SHIRLEY. Me? Oh I'd love to but...

(whispers)

I have no talent.

AQUA MARIE. Well I just heard you sing, and girl, you can *wail.*

(tosses her hair)

CAPT. KING. *(enters, speaking on his shell-phone)* "Act now, and with each purchase get an adorable Teddy Bear Hamster. You should see them work that wheel!...Aye Long John Gold, we ship to Broadway. See you at the Grand Opening."

(hands the phone to **AQUA***)*

Oh that Long John Gold is an earful, don't you...have legs? You're a were-maid? Ahh!!! All hands on deck! All hands on deck –

(As **AQUA** *helps our* **HEROES** *escape,* **PIRATES** *race in, and place the palms of their hands upon the stage.)*

All hands on...It's an expression you-nincompoop-decks. Seize them! And this time, make them walk the plank.

HOAGY. *(peaking out from behind his hiding place)* Yeah!

(He is pulled into safety by **SHIRLEY***.)*

PIRATE PEARL. But Captain, the runway be freshly painted for me fashion show.

PIRATE JADE. Then like, feed them to a velociraptor.

PIRATE RUBY. Hello, raptors be extinct.

CAPT. KING. Then sink them in quicksand, I don't know!

OTHER PIRATES. Quicksand? There's no quicksand on this island,

(Actually say:)

Etc., ad lib.

(They start to "sink," as our **HEROES** *escape. Sound Cue: phone.)*

CAPT. KING. *(answering his phone)* "Endangered Species Are-Long John Gold? Your deluxe mermaid package will be-running late are ye?...You want to catch the big show, I understand."

MARY JANE TRAPPER. (*urgently enters*) "Big Show!?"

> (*Using* **MARY** *as leverage, the other* **PIRATES** *escape their quicksand fate, and clump around their* **CAPT.** *Following on tip-toe, as he paces.*)

CAPT. KING. (*covering the receiver to yell at his fleet*) Why didn't someone tell me there was going to be a talent competition?!

BARNACLE JILL. (*searching the ground thru her scope*) Check out the moon.

SALMAGUNDI. (*shifting Jill's scope to the sky*) Tis a lunar blue!

MARY JANE TRAPPER. Like me very own follow-spot.

PIRATES. (*moonstruck*) Oooo…..

CAPT. KING. (*still on the phone*) "And you expect *whom* to perform?"

> (**PIRATES** *mime: "Ooh, Me, me, and me! Pick me!" etc.*)

"The Big Mermaid?"

> (**PIRATES** *groan in disappointment.* **CAPT.** *muffles the receiver.*)

She'll pack endangered species in for twenty leagues. They'll come crawling and jumping and slithering out of the jungle to see her, and that is when –

CRUSHER. We'll capture the whole lot of 'em!

CAPT. KING. Aye.

(*back on phone*)

"Fear not Long John Gold, your belting mermaid will be on the boards as advertised. Aye…Aye…Aye" – (*Hangs up.*) Yi Yi; that Long John Gold is more taxing than the Mary Jane Trapper.

(*exiting*)

Vex me now!

MARY JANE TRAPPER. I've got costumes in the ship, I'm gonna' put on a swell show!

CRUSHER. You 'eard the Cap'n, no one enters that competition except the bloody mermaid.

PIRATE DIVAS. Ew.

MARY JANE TRAPPER. Pssst! Me hearties...

(All huddle around her as she whispers.)

Between you and me and the crow's nest: The Cap'n... has issues.

OTHER PIRATES. Ooh.

MARY JANE TRAPPER. He's a jellyfish! Envious of me, "our," talent. A serious maritime discretion.

OTHER PIRATES. *Ooh.*

JACK DUSTY. *(referring to the piratical article page of the storybook)* "No El Capitan may prevent a buccaneer from appearing in a talent competition."

MARY JANE TRAPPER. What did I tell thee? Now let's get to work. I've got a show to do!

(PIRATES *enthusiastically scatter to rehearse.)*

Ye shall be me back-up dancers.

MIRAGE. We've got our own act.

MARY JANE TRAPPER. Pirate Pearl will mend me costume. I can see it now: Sequins, feathers, a mad splash of glitter!

(cackles like a mad scientist, then is struck with further inspiration)

TWINKLE TOES. Is there a Bedazzler on deck?!

MARY JANE TRAPPER. *(exiting followed by a dancing* **TWINKLE***)* Oh Captain me Captain, can I borrow your Bedazzler?!

SALAMAGUNDI. So me mateys; what be our act?

BUBBA THE PIRATE. I can tell jokes!...Did you hear about the new pirate movie? It's rated: aRgh!

(The **CREW** *is not amused.)*

Wait! I got me another: How many pirates does it take to screw in a light bulb? None.
We use torches. Argh!...? Okay, why did the pirate cross the sea?...Because he was a pirate, argh.

OTHER PIRATES. *(after a pause, get it)* Argh!!

(pat each other on the back, high-five, etc.)

BARNACLE JILL. Let's form a band.

SABERTOOTH. But we already be a band of pirates.

PIRATE RUBY. Hello. You just need a new name.

JACK DUSTY. 'In *Stink?*'

BARNACLE JILL. "The Bloody Skulls?"

SCURVY. 'I've Got Scurvy!'

PIRATE PEARL. Nay. Too punk. Something more commercial. Like, 'The Back *Fleet* Boys.'

BARNACLE JILL. But I be a girl.

JACK DUSTY. 'The Back Fleet *Pirates?*'

OTHER PIRATES. 'The Back Fleet Pirates?' Huzzah!

(**PARROT** *echoes: "Huzzah."*)

BARNACLE JILL. Wait, wait. What shall our broadside ballad be?

CAPT. KING. *(enters)* Ooh that Mary Jane Trapper's *walking the plank of my patience.*

SALMAGUNDI. That's it!

BUBBA THE PIRATE. Capt. King, wanna' be in our band?

CAPT. KING. I told you: No one is to…

BARNACLE JILL. You can sing lead?

CAPT. KING. *(without missing a beat)* Where's my music?!

(*As a* **PIRATE** *hands him sheet music, the* **CAPT.** *continues his exit followed by the* **CREW.** *Sound Cue: VOLCANIC RUMBLE.* **AQUA & SHIRLEY** *stagger from their hiding place.*)

AQUA. *(out of breath)* Slow down girl, I'm not used to gams.

SHIRLEY. That's okay. If I had fins, I'd finally make the swim team…

(*Sound Cue: VOLCANIC RUMBLE.* **AQUA** *falls.* **SHIRLEY** *helps* **AQUA** *to her new found feet.*)

Don't worry Aqua. If the island sinks, you can come live with me! My neighbors have a sprinkler.

AQUA. You're so lucky.

SHIRLEY. Me? I have to hold my nose underwater. But you…Oh –

(SONG #06: 'WHOEVER YOU ARE')

SHIRLEY.

IF I WERE YOU

AQUA.

AND YOU WERE ME

AQUA.	**SHIRLEY.**
IMAGINE HOW WONDERFUL	IMAGINE THE WONDERFUL
LIFE WOULD BE	THINGS I COULD SEE

SHIRLEY.

I WISH I WAS A MERMAID, I'D SAIL TO GREET THE MORN
UPON THE WAKE OF DOLPHINS! WIND AT MY BACK AIR
   BORNE
DIVING FOR LOST TREASURE I'D FIND THE PERFECT PEARL
IF I WAS A MERMAID GIRL

AQUA.

IF ONLY I WERE HUMAN I'D DANCE UPON TWO LEGS
AND SLEEP UPON A PILLOW, INSTEAD OF A SEA BED
I WOULDN'T SWIM IN SCHOOLS YET LEARN ABOUT THE
   WORLD
IF I WERE A REAL LIVE GIRL

SHIRLEY.

BUT IF I WERE YOU

AQUA.

AND YOU WERE ME

BOTH.

WE'D HAVE NEVER CROSSED THE OCEAN
TO WHERE WE WERE MEANT TO BE

AQUA & ENDANGERED SPECIES. *(the latter watching from afar)*

SO, INSTEAD OF ALWAYS WISHING
YOU ARE SOMETHING YOU ARE NOT
KNOW EVERYTHING YOU ENVY IS EVERYTHING YOU'VE GOT

AQUA.

YOU CAN MAKE A SPLASH WITHOUT WATER

SHIRLEY.

YOU CAN WAVE YOUR ARMS TO DANCE

ALL.

AND IF BY CHANCE YOU'RE LEFT WONDERING WHO –
-EVER YOU (EVER YOU ARE) ARE
WHO EVER (WHO EVER YOU ARE) YOU ARE
WHO EVER YOU ARE

AQUA.

LET IT BE YOU...

Come on Shirley, we've got a show to do.

(LIGHT CUE: FADE TO BLACK. INTERMISSION, or SEGUE to next scene.)

ACT TWO

THE WACKY TACKY IDOL COMPETITIONS

(SETTING: The foot of the volcano.)

(AT RISE: In route to the show-within-the show, characters enter through the audience:)

MARY JANE TRAPPER. *(to* **TWINKLE***)* Stop following me!

TWINKLE TOES. *(to* **BUBBA***)* Stop following me!

*(***PARROT** *repeats "Stop following me.")*

MCCAW. Stop repeating after me!

*(***PARROT***: "Stop repeating after me.")*

BUBBA. *(to his new comedy* **PARTNER***)* Let's go over the punch line again.

*(***PRIMATES** *enter being chased by* **SABERTOOTH &** **CRUSHER** *brandishing a net. Light/Sound Cue: American Idol Pastiche. All exit as* **HOAGY** *enters thru the curtains with a prop microphone to host Wacky Tacky Idol.)*

HOAGY. Thank you; thank you, ladies and gentleman and creatures of all species. Welcome to Wacky Tacky Idol. Is everybody wacky?!…That's nice. Okay, well I know you were expecting Ryan Seaweed to host. But ah… pparently he's disappeared. Along with our judges: Randy the Dawg-Fish and Simon the Shark. So, I volunteered to MC, and the *volcano* has graciously agreed to be this season's guest judge.

(Sound Cue: VOLCANIC RUMBLE which sends **HOAGY** *reeling.)*

[And you thought Simon was tough.] Now let's get things swinging with our first contestants: The Apes of Monkey Beach!

(SONG #07: 'MONKEY SEE / MONKEY DO')

PRIMATES.
MONKEY SEE / MONKEY DO
DO GOOD AND GOOD WILL FOLLOW YOU
OH, MONKEY SEE GOOD, GOOD MONKEY DO

SOME CREATURES DO WHATEVER THEY SEE
THEY DON'T USE THEIR MINDS
SOME FOLKS REFUSE TO LIVE AND LET BREATHE
THEY CAN BE UNKIND
SET AN AMPLE EXAMPLE FOR US TO HEED
IF YOU DO A GOOD DEED MAYBE WE WILL FOLLOW YOUR
    LEAD
A-one-two-three –
MONKEY SEE / MONKEY DO
DO GOOD AND GOOD WILL FOLLOW YOU
OH, MONKEY SEE GOOD / GOOD MONKEY –

Hey Monkey You're So Fine
Up There Swingin' On A Vine
Hey Monkey, Hey Monkey!

(encouraging the audience to clap along)

Hey Monkey You're So Fine
Up There Swingin' On A Vine
Hey Monkey, Hey Monkey!

SABERTOOTH & CRUSHER. *(sneaking up on the* **APES** *with a net)*
Hey Monkey You're so Fine
Gonna' Catch you, Call You Mine
Hey Monkey Hey Monkey!

(They capture the **APES**, *sweeping them offstage.)*

BABY MONKEY. Hey!

*(**SONG #08: 'MONKEY BEACH.'** The* **COOL CAT BAND** *play inflatable instruments.)*

COOL CATS.
TIME TO GO WHERE THE COOL CATS GROW –
UP ON MONKEY BEACH

LET'S HANG TEN WITH ORANGUTAN FRIENDS
DOWN ON MONKEY BEACH
WHAT COULD BE MORE FUN THAN A BARREL FULL OF
    MONKEY'S
BARRELING A TUBULAR WAVE?
COWABUNGA WITH BABOONS ON A BOOGIE BOARD
GO BANANAS ON MONKEY BEACH
SWING ON A VINE LIKE IT'S A BUNGEE CHORD
CAMP A CABANA ON MONKEY BEACH
FUN IS ALWAYS IN REACH, SURF'S UP!
IT'S ALWAYS SUMMER ON MONKEY BEACH
SURF'S UP!
IT'S ALWAYS SUMMER ON MONKEY BEACH
SURF'S UP!
IT'S ALWAYS SUMMER ON MONKEY BEACH
WIPE OUT!

HOAGY. Thank you for like, that totally gnarly and boda-cious tune. And now, for our next Wacky Tacky contestant: Salmagundi.

SALMAGUNDI. With me partner in interruptive dance: Barnacle Jill.

JACK DUSTY. *(reads from the storybook)*
    'There Once Was a Sailor Named Liam,
    Who Plundered a Pirate Mu*seum*
    Then Acted All Snooty, Till He Lost All His Booty
    In The Ca*rib*bean, [Or Is It Pronounced, 'Carib*bean*?']
    And then he got eaten by a shark.

    (Closes the book and exits as **SAL** *mimes getting eaten by a shark.)*

HOAGY. Thank you. Whatever that was. It certainly was 'dramatical.' [If not a tad disturbing]. And now it's time for:

SCURVY JO. *(enthusiastically takes the stage)* Scurvy Jo, and I've got Scurvy!

    (to **PIANIST***, suddenly very serious)*

    Maestro…

(SONG #09: 'THE SCURVY LITTLE DITTY')

ON A SHIP WITHOUT NO CITRUS
'CEPT ONCE A YEAR AT CHRISTMAS
AN ORANGE IN ME STOCKING
THAT MUST LAST ME ALL YEAR LONG
THOUGH IT MAY NOT BE RIGHT PRETTY
I SING THIS SCURVY DITTY
SO TAKE YOUR VITAMINS A THRU Z
CAUSE SCURVY BE THE LACK OF VITAMIN C!

(proudly)

Never in my life have I taken a lesson.

HOAGY. Thank you Scurvy Jo for that educational ditty. I will be sure to eat an orange. And now –

PIRATE PEARL. *(enters sporting a fabulous new getup)* A word from our sponsor: No pirate wardrobe is complete without a swashbuckling ensemble from the Pirate Pearl Spring Collection, inspired by Blue *Weave* the Pirate.

(Sound Cue: Runway music underscore: **DIVAS** *enter in blue wigs modeling Pearl's latest creations.)*

Notice the striking silhouette on skull & crossbones motif-navy being this year's blue. Work it, work it. Our next model is sporting the latest in galley wear: a kettle doubling as a jaunty cap. Good for home or mutiny.

PIRATE RUBY. It's hot.

PIRATE PEARL. Thanks.

PIRATE RUBY. No I mean really, it's hot. I can't breath.

PIRATE PEARL. Ho hum. Such is the price of fashion. Our next model is wearing a lovely dead buzzard on her head. What daring, what artistry, what couture! You too can be America's Next Top Pirate with a Pirate Pearl original. [Available wherever good taste is plundered.]

(having worked the runway, the **DIVAS** *exit)*

HOAGY. And now back to our show. Let's give a Wacky Tacky Welcome to:

BUBBA THE PIRATE. *(enters)* Jolly Dodger here with my partner in comedy! "What's the difference between Celine Dion and a Great white Shark?"

PARTNER IN COMEDY. One is a French-Canadian singer, and the other, an ocean predator.

BUBBA THE PIRATE. Genius!

MARY JANE TRAPPER. *(storming the stage)* Next!

TWINKLE TOES. Next!

BUBBA THE PIRATE. *(passes the microphone as he exits)* I get no respect.

(SONG #10: 'PIRATES & PARROTS')

MCCAW. *(and two other **PIRATES**)* McCaw 'ere with me best friend Polly.

(**PARROT:** *"But me stage name is 'Pollywood.'"*)

PIRATES AND PARROTS GO TOGETHER
LIKE BIRDS OF A FEATHER
YOU CAN GIVE A PARROT A SHOULDER TO LEAN ON
AND IN RETURN SHE'LL PECK YOU WITH HER BEAK

(**PARROT** *pecks too hard.*)

Ow!

THAT IS WHY ME BEST FRIEND IS A BIRD

MCCAW & FRIENDS.

POLLY CAN AIRMAIL YOUR MATE A MESSAGE
OVER ROUGH AND BUBBLING WATERS AS THEY TOIL
SHE'LL MIGRATE WITH HER MATES FROM SEDATE VACATION
IN SAINT ROYAL

PIRATES AND PARROTS GO TOGETHER
THEY REPEAT EVERY UTTERANCE THAT YOU ARRGH

(**PARROT:** *"Argh!"*)

ARRGH!
BENEATH A CANOPY OF TREES
THEY TWEET IN PERFECT HARMONY
THAT'S WHY ME BEST FRIEND IS A BIRD, YO HO HO
A PIRATES BEST FRIEND IS HIS BIRD

(**PARROT***: "Land ho!"*)

YA KNOW A PIRATES BEST FRIEND IS FOR THE BIRDS!

HOAGY. And now friends, the one and only –

THE MARY JANE TRAPPER. Me!!

HOAGY. Back Fleet Pirates!

(SONG #11: 'THE BALLAD OF MARY JANE' **MARY JANE** *exits as the* **CAPT.** *leads a* **PIRATICAL QUINTET,** *who enter with chairs to execute their 'Boy Band' choreography.)*

CAPT. KING.

ADRIFT UPON THE OCEAN WITH A SECOND CLASS FIRST
　　MATE

SOLO.

You have no class!

CAPT. KING.

WHO CAN'T FATHOM THE SLIGHTEST NOTION
OF HOW HER VOICE GRATES
OH MARY CAN'T YOU SEE?
YOU ARE NOT THE BOSS OF ME
YOU ARE

QUINTET.

WALKING THE PLANK OF MY PATIENCE MARY JANE
I AM DIVING OFF THE DEEP END, GIRL
YOU ARE DRIVING ME INSANE, MARY JANE
MARY JANE

SOLO.

Always on the attack –

Why you gotta' act, like you're always all that?

SOLO.

It's a shame 'cause you could be a great leader
If you could just reign it in, and I could-just rhyme
'leader'

QUINTET.

OH MARY CAN'T YOU SEE?
YOU ARE NOT THE BOSS OF ME!
YOU ARE –
WALKING THE PLANK OF MY PATIENCE MARY JANE
(I AM) DIVING OFF THE DEEP END

YOU ARE DRIVING ME INSANE
MARY JANE, (PIRATE GIRL)
YOU'RE WORKING… *(vocal ad lib)* MY VERY LAST NERVE!

MARY JANE TRAPPER. Ooh that be a fine sea shanty mateys. Can you write one about me?! Hit it!

(SONG #12: THE PIRATICAL TAP)

MARY JANE TRAPPER.

Ahoy There Mateys, Can't You See?
I'm The Sailor Who Can Dance Cross The Seven Seas!
TAP TAP TAP TAP
I'M THE PIRATE WITH THE KNACK FOR PIRATICAL TAP
TAP TAP TAP TAP
I'M THE PIRATE WITH THE KNACK FOR PIRATICAL TAP
Break it Down!

Be Ye Mermaid Bird Am*phib*ian
Buccaneer, Pirate *Of* The Caribbean
No One On Water Is A Better Tapper
Than Me: '*M-*Trap!'

TWINKLE TOES. Mary Jane Trapper! "So you think you can dance-dance dance"

MARY JANE TRAPPER.

TAP TAP TAP TAP
I'M THE PIRATE WITH THE KNACK FOR PIRATICAL TAP
TAP TAP TAP TAP, I'M…

(PIRATES *tap on with a net to dance* **MARY** *Offstage.* **SEGUE: SONG #13: THE PIRATICAL RAP.'** **TOMMY PIPES** *enters.)*

TOMMY PIPES. Wuz up wacky Tacky Boo?!… I said: Wuz up wacky Tacky Bo?!
Give me a beat!

(His Hip-Hop **CREW** *enters, creating a vocal beat box.)*
MARY JANE IS A TAPPER, BUT THIS SAILOR IS A RAPPER
SO LISTEN UP MATEYS GOTTA' LESSON TO LEARN
IF YOU WANT TO BE A PIRATE FROM BOW TO STERN

(gestures)

TOMMY PIPES. *(cont.)*
> STARBOARDS' TO THE RIGHT
> PORT IS ON THE LEFT
> YOU BETTER KNOW THIS TO PASS THE PIRATE TEST:
> A 'GALLEY' IS A KITCHEN, A 'BRIG' IS A JAIL
> IF THE SHIP IS HOLDING WATER, YO! BETTER GRAB A PAIL!
> STARBOARDS' TO THE RIGHT, PORT IS ON THE LEFT
> YOU BETTER KNOW THIS TO PASS THE PIRATE TEST:

BEAT PIRATE SOLO.
> 'CAREEN' IS HOW YOU CLEAN, THE BOTTOM OF A SHIP

BEAT PIRATE SOLO.
> A 'CAT-O-NINE TAIL'S IS NOT A CAT IT IS A WHIP

TOMMY & CREW.
> STARBOARDS' TO THE RIGHT, PORT IS ON THE LEFT
> YOU BETTER KNOW THIS TO PASS THE PIRATE TEST:

TOMMY PIPES.
> TO 'GIVE QUARTER' IS HOLD MERCY WHEN A PRISONER
>   PLEAS
> A CODE FOR FELLOW PIRATES IS TO SAY

TOMMY & CREW.
> 'I'M FROM THE SEA!"

> *(repeating Tommy's choreography)*

> STARBOARDS' TO THE RIGHT
> PORT IS ON THE LEFT
> YOU BETTER KNOW THIS TO PASS THE PIRATE TEST:

> *(They teach the audience the refrain:)*

> STARBOARD'S TO THE RIGHT
> PORT IS ON THE LEFT
> YOU BETTER KNOW THIS TO PASS THE PIRATE TEST'

> *(dance break)*

> GO SCURVY, GO SCURVY
> GO SCURVY IT'S YOUR BIRTHDAY
> GO SCURVY, GO SCURVY
> GO SCURVY IT'S YOUR BIRTHDAY

> YO HO HO HO AND A BOTTLE OF FUN

TOMMY PIPES. Thank you Wacky Tacky!

SCURVY JO. Thank you Cleveland!

(They carry him off.)

Cleveland Rocks!

(*LIGHT CUE: MEANWHILE 'BACKSTAGE':*)

SHIRLEY. What do you mean you've lost your voice?!

AQUA MARIE. Too much pollution.

(coughs)

HOAGY. Don't stress Aqua, you'll get Ick. Rest your gills. Shirley will go on for you.

SHIRLEY. She will?

AQUA. Make it quick kid, I've got fins' sprouting here!

SHIRLEY. *(panicking)* But I…don't have a costume!?

HOAGY. Break a fin.

*(Tosses **SHIRLEY** her boa.)*

AQUA MARIE. *(crowning **SHIRLEY** with her tiara)* And remember: You're going out there a mermaid, but you're coming back a *star*fish!

(Light cue: crossfade: Meanwhile, onstage:)

HOAGY. Ladies and gentleman, it's the moment you've all been waiting for: The Merminator herself. Your current Wacky Tacky title holder, The Big Mermaid, Aqua Ma –

SHIRLEY. Stall!

HOAGY. But *first*! – um…a word from…The Bard:

(Clears throat, then recites from 'Midsummer's Night Dream'.)

'Once I sat upon a promontory and heard a mermaid uttering such dulcet and harmonious breath –"

SHIRLEY. I'm not ready yet!!

HOAGY. Which reminds me of a song:

SHIRLEY HAD A LITTLE LAMB
LITTLE LAMB, LITTLE LAMB
SHIRLEY HAD A LITTLE LAMB
ITS FLEECE WAS –[I'm dyin' out here] – SNOW.

(He coaxes a tentative **SHIRLEY** *from the wings for an acapella reprise of:)*

SHIRLEY.

I'M A BIG OLE MERMAID. S.C.A.R.E.D.?
THAT'S ME –

SCURVY JO. *(poking his head out from behind the curtain)* Sing out Shirley, sing out!

SHIRLEY.

A BIG OLE MERMAID, M.E.R.M.A.I.D.
SWEETER THA A SHARK, CUTER THAN A WHALE
A SEAWEED SIREN WHO SINGS IT'S TIME TO TELL THE TALE
OF THIS BIG OLD MERMAID M.E.R.M.A.I.D

*(**SONG #14: 'SHAKE THAT FIN!'** **FLAMINGO DANCERS** enter forming a 'Girl Group'.)*

FLAMINGOS.

COME SET SAIL UPON THE GAIL OF IMAGINATION EARTH
IF YOU DREAM IT YOU CAN ACHIEVE IT
ALL IT TAKES IS A LITTLE WORK
CATCH A CURL BABY, CELEBRATE YOUR WORTH!

GET UP AND: SHAKE SHAKE THAT FIN, SHAKE IT BABY
BABY SHAKE THAT FIN
SHAKE SHAKE THAT FIN, SHAKE IT BABY
WHY SINK WHEN YOU CAN SWIM?
GET UP AND SHAKE THAT *FIN!*

SHIRLEY.

WHEN THE RIDE IS RESTLESS
AND YOUR TALE'S TOO TWISTED TO MOVE
THE TIDE'S AGAINST YOU
AND ITS CREST IS STRESSIN' YOUR GROOVE
KEEP ON TREADING WATER, TIMES' TOO PRECIOUS TO LOSE

SHIRLEY & THE FLAMINGOS.

GET UP AND: SHAKE SHAKE THAT FIN, SHAKE IT BABY
BABY SHAKE THAT FIN
SHAKE SHAKE THAT FIN, SHAKE IT BABY
WHY SINK WHEN YOU CAN SWIM?
GET UP AND SHAKE THAT *FIN!*

FLAMINGOS.

GO MERMAID GO MERMAID GO BIG OLE MERMAID
SHAKE YOUR IMAGINATION MERMAID SHAKE THAT FIN
GO MERMAID GO MERMAID GO BIG OLE MERMAID
SHAKE YOUR IMAGINATION SURLEY SHAKE THAT FIN

SHIRLEY & THE FLAMINGOS.

YES, SHAKE SHAKE THAT FIN SHAKE IT BABY
BABY SHAKE THAT FIN
SHAKE SHAKE THAT FIN SHAKE IT BABY
WHY SINK WHEN YOU CAN SWIM,
GET UP AND SHAKE THAT FIN
SHAKE, SHAKE THAT FIN, GET UP AND SHAKE THAT FIN!

(Sound Cue: VOLCANIC RUMBLE. Save for the **CAPT., CONTESTANTS** *urgently enter.)*

THE MARY JANE TRAPPER. *(with a mic)* This is Mary Jane Trapper reporting live from Wacky Tacky Boo, thanking all my lucky fans for choosing *me* to be your next Wacky Tacky Idol.

(Sound Cue: VOLCANIC RUMBLE)

SHIRLEY. *(seizing the mic)* The volcano wants a recount.

(SHIRLEY *addresses the audience as other* **CONTESTANTS** *work the crowd for their vote.)*

SHIRLEY. By round of applause, who will be your next Wacky Tacky Idol?

(Music Cue: TREMOLO)

Will it be act number one: The Primates?

(She continues thru the running order, with each of the acts hawking the audience for votes.)

…The Mermaid understudy?

CAPT. KING. *(enters)* Stop this charade! *(pronounced "sha-rad")* This is no mermaid!

(Sound Cue: VOLCANIC ERUPTION)

SALMAGUNDI. The volcano, she's erupting!

SHIRLEY. Quick, make an offering!

CAPT. KING. *(grabbing the mic, asks an audience member)* How much for the shoes, they're fabulous?

SHIRLEY. To the volcano!

> *(***BABY MONKEY** *and other* **PRIMATES** *shuffle in, disguised as* **LONG JOHN GOLD***, either in a huddle, or with one actor on another's shoulder-the tallest wearing a pirate hat a gold cape around them.)*

'LONG JOHN GOLD' #1. Stop the show!

BARNACLE JILL. *(seeing him thru her spyglass)* Long John Gold!

PIRATES. Huzzah!

BABY MONKEY. *(pokes out from under the cape)* It's working?

> *(Other* **PRIMATES** *shush her/him as he hides back under the cape.)*

'LONG JOHN GOLD' #2. The volcano's not erupting. She is applauding.

'LONG JOHN GOLD' #1. A starfish is born!

'LONG JOHN GOLD' #2. That singing starfish is a sensation! [Or something like that].

MARY JANE TRAPPER. What about me?

> *(Other* **PIRATES** *chime in: 'Me?!')*

'LONG JOHN GOLD' #3. All of ye belong in the business of show.

MARY JANE TRAPPER. Is it just me, or does Long John Gold have three heads?

TWINKLE TOES. And a tail.

'LONG JOHN GOLD' #1. Now now, let's all look past our differences and work together to um, combine fleets and…

MARY JANE TRAPPER. Put on a show?!

> *(faints)*

SHIRLEY. Hoagy can write the music!

PIRATE PEARL. I'll make the costumes.

MARY JANE TRAPPER. *(popping her head up)* And I'll direct.

> *(faints)*

CAPT. KING. Oh that Mary Jane Trapper is such a diva. Everyone in the biz knows he who steers the ship; directs the show.

MIRAGE. *I* steer the ship Captain. Does that mean that…

(**PIRATES** *argue.*)

SHIRLEY. At ease mateys! We must all work together to plunder naught but our *imaginations*. Therein lays the treasure!

PIRATES. What, no gold?

HOAGY. Unearth your artistic buried treasure, and play a leading role in Mother Nature's show!

PIRATE PEARL. Hip hop –

OTHER PIRATES. (*as in 'Huzzah!'*) Bizarre!

(**PARROT**: *"Or something like that."*)

SHIRLEY. [Or something like that.]

HOAGY. And our first production shall be?

MARY JANE TRAPPER. 'The Mary Jane Trapper Christmas Spectacular?'

TWINKLE TOES. "High School Musical?!"

SHIRLEY. Nay: The Pirate Musical!

ALL. "The Pirate Musical!" Huzzah!

(*All exit except:*)

BABY MONKEY. Needs a better title.

EPILOGUE

NARRATOR. *(once again reading from the storybook)* "And so, the pollution pirates cleaned up their act and released all the animals, while Shirley and Hoagy caught a curl to *(town of production)*. Captain King transformed his floating pet shop into a *show boat* which staged, "The Pirate Musical!" Not only did Bubba finally embrace his name, he managed to tell an actual joke. Scurvy changed *his* name to *Healthy* Jo and The Big Mermaid did a water ballet. The Volcano was so pleased with her green new island; she stopped having anger management issues and provided rhythm for the big finale:

ALL. Bongo in The Congo!!

(SONG #15: 'BONGO IN THE CONGO!')

ANIMALS. *(enter in festive costumes)*
> LET'S GO BONGO IN THE CONGO MOVE YOUR BURNIN'
>   FEET
> RUMBA TO THEE DRUM OF A RHYTHMIC ISLAND BEAT
> IF YE HEAD BE HOT WITH LAVA BEFORE YOUR TOP
>   EXPLODES
> GO BONGO IN THE CONGO AND DANCE AWAY YOUR WOES,
>   ARGH!!

PIRATE MEN.
> WHEN I WAS A WEE PIRATE ME CAPTAIN SAID TO ME
> 'REMEMBER LAND HO! WHILST NAVIGATING ROUGH SEAS
> DREAM OF LUSH PARADISE, LIKE (DR.) LIVINGSTON I
>   PRESUME
> AND SHOULD YOUR PEACE OF MIND MUTINY
> COMMANDEER THIS HAPPY TUNE:

PIRATE WOMEN.
> 'GO BONGO IN THE CONGO MOVE YOUR BURNIN' FEET
> RUMBA TO THEE DRUM OF A RHYTHMIC ISLAND BEAT
> IF YE HEAD BE HOT WITH LAVA BEFORE YOUR TOP
>   EXPLODES
> GO BONGO IN THE CONGO!
> (ALL ECHO: 'BONGO IN THE CONGO!')
> AND DANCE AWAY YOUR WOES, ARGH!!

ANIMALS.

GO BONGO, BONGO IN THE CONGO WE'LL GO

PIRATES.

BONGO.... BONGO IN THE CONGO WE'LL GO...
BONGO IN THE CONGO, CONGA TO THE BONGO –

ANIMALS.

BONGO IN THE CONGO, CONGA TO THE BONGO –
CONGA TO THE BONGO IN THE CONGO, HEY HEY HEY!

(dance break)

IF YE HEAD BE HOT WITH LAVA BEFORE YOUR TOP
    EXPLODES
GO BONGO IN THE CONGO (BONGO IN THE CONGO!)
AND DANCE AWAY (DANCE AWAY YOUR) YOUR WOES
AND DANCE AWAY YOUR WOES: ARGH!!

*(LIGHT CUE: BLACKOUT…CURTAIN CALL-
MUSIC CUE: BONGO: REPRISE:)*

COMPANY.

IF YE HEAD BE HOT WITH LAVA BEFORE YOUR TOP
    EXPLODES
GO BONGO IN THE CONGO (BONGO IN THE CONGO!)
AND DANCE AWAY (DANCE AWAY YOUR) YOUR WOES
AND DANCE AWAY YOUR WOES: ARGH!!

End

APPENDIX A
Stage Craft

SCENERY

With the primary action of the musical unfolding on the island of imagination, locations may be suggested with moveable boxes or stairs – painted with neon orange and pink animal printed sides, others with neon green and aqua skull & crossbones – accented in black, scattered in front of a neon backdrop, framed with palm trees and hanging neon vines.

COSTUMES

SHIRLEY & HOAGY: Like Indiana Jones on a Hawaiian vacation.

THE ENDANGERED SPECIES: Base costumes (such as overalls), each with a distinct color or pattern befitting their species, enhanced with appropriate neon accessories, (monkey ears and tails, cat glasses, and feathered boas, etc.)

THE PIRATES: Classic swashbuckling attire mixed-matched with neon gear, as if pillaged from trashcans and theatre trunks.

THE MERMAID: A sequined dress, "seaweed boa" made of artificial ivy garland entwined with random debris.

PROPS

Backpacks: (2), Butterfly Net, 'Endangered Species 'R Us' flyers: (*on neon paper to crumble and throw*), Eyeglasses, Field Journal and pencil, Fishing Net, Flowered Garland

Gold Cape, Gummy Worms, Magnifying Glass, Message in a Bottle

Microphone: (*hand prop for show-within-the show*), Life Preserver, Ocean Debris: (*including a plastic soda-pack ring*), Parrot Puppet (*or stuffed animal*), Practical Pirate Swords (2), Rolling Pin, Seaweed Boa, "Shell-ular" Phone, Spy Glass., Storybook

SOUND EFFECTS

Volcanic Rumble, Various underscore and pre-show music.

APPENDIX B
Study Guide / Piratical Glossary

AFOUL: *Entangled.*

AFT: *Towards the STERN or rear (poop deck) of the ship.*

ALOOF: *To sail close to the wind.*

BALLAST: *Stones or other objects placed at the ship's bottom for balance.*

BILGE: *Lowest level of a ship's hull.*

BINNACLE: *Wooden box which holds the ship's log (journal) et. al.*

BOOTY: *Gold, jewels, grain, medicine, and spices which were popular treasures.*

BRIG: *The ship's jail.*

BUCCANEERS: *Pirates of the Caribbean who dried or "boucan" meat.*

BURIED TREASURE: *For the most part, a romantic myth.*

CAREEN: *To scrape barnacles from the ships hull.*

CODE: *Articles which govern a particular ship. Despite the rowdy reputation of pirates, such rules of conduct were democratic in drafting, and THE PIRATE MUSICAL! company should be encouraged to create their own.*

CROW's NEST: *Ships observation perch.*

CRUSHER: *The ship's policeman.*

DAVY JONES: *Mythical spirit who governs drowned pirates and sailors.*

DINGY: *A ship's row boat.*

DOUBLOONS: *Gold coins*

FORE: *Towards the front (or BOW) of the ship.*

FEMALE PIRATES: *There were quite a few, often disguised as men.*

FROM THE SEA: *A pirate password between two ships.*

GALLEON: *Speedy, Spanish cargo vessel, usually heavily armed.*

GALLEY: *A ship's kitchen.*

GALLOWS: *A wooden platform for hanging*

GOVERNOR: *The ruler of an English, French, or Spanish colony, who had the authority of his home country's King or Queen.*

HUZZAH!: *Salutations*

JACK DUSTY: *The keeper of a ship's records.*

JAUNTY: *To swagger about.*

LETTER OF MARQUE: *An official license granting a Captain permission to plunder.*

JOLLY ROGER: *A skull & crossed bones flag.*

MAROON: *To desert on shore.*

NO QUARTER: *Take no prisoners/show no mercy.*

ON THE ACCOUNT: *Code phrase for the "occupation" of pirating.*

PIECES OF EIGHT: *Spanish silver coins cut into eight bits, and accepted as legal currency in Colonial America.*

PIRATE: *Name assigned by The Greeks to those who plundered trade ships.*

PIRATE ARTICLES: *List of pirate protocol/Code of Conduct.(See CODE)*

PIRATE FLAGS: *Created and flown to identify a ship belonging to an allegiance of pirates, as oppose to a specific country.*

PORT: *The left side of the ship.*

PORT ROYAL: *A Pirate haven in the Caribbean, now underwater. Another such 'hangout' was Madagascar, which was said to be particularly rowdy.*

PRIZE: *Captured cargo.*

PRIVATEERS: *A sailor hired by royalty to attack and rob enemy ships.*

PIERCING YOUR EAR: *Believed to improve eye-sight.*

QUARTER: *Mercy, freedom.*

QUARTERMASTER: *The highest ranking crew member voted by his/her peers.*

RED ALERT: *A red flag signaling a pirate attack, with no mercy.*

RUM RAT: *A pirate who drinks too much.*

RUNNING THE GAUNTLET: *A form of punishment .*

SALMAGUNDI: *A pirate's favorite cold dish.*

SALTY DOG: *An insulting name.*

SCURVY: *Common sailor's disease brought about by lack of vitamin C.*

SCUTTLEBUTT: *Gossip. Often shared round the ship's scuttle, or water casket.*

SHARE OUT: *The act of dividing loot.*

SHIP NAMES: *Often changed to avoid identification.*

SKEDADDLE: *To sneak away when one should be working.*

SLOPS: *Ill-fitting, "sloppy" clothing sold by the ship's Purser.*

STARBOARD: *The right side of a ship.*

STRANDED: *To run aground on a sandbar or beach.*

TOMMY PIPES: *Slang for boats man.*

WAFT: *Distress signal flown atop a ship's mast.*

WALKING THE PLANK: *Pirate myth perpetuated by Hollywood.*

APPENDIX C
Study Guide

Seven fun projects to make the most of your adventure!

1) **PIRATICAL ARTICLES**
   Have your cast and crew draft their own our "Pirate Code," a contract
   of what is expected of them as an artistic team setting sail on a creative
   voyage.

2) **GLOSSARY**
   Use the glossary of piratical terms to create new pirate names. Re-
   search and add terms of your own. A fun creative tool we used in Peter
   Pan was to have each pirate pick a word and use that word somewhere
   when required by the text to adlib.

3) **CHARACTER BIOGRAPHY'S**
   Write a brief biography about your character answering such ques-
   tions as:
   Who am I? What is my occupation? What are my goals, fears, dreams?

4) **FACT vs. FICTION**
   While there are elements of *The Pirate Musical* based upon histori-
   cal facts, most of this play employs myth and imagination. Which is
   which? For example, did pirates actually walk the plank? Which animals are endangered? Which species co-habitat with each other in
   real if and which do not?

5) **GO GREEN!**
   Make your production eco-friendly by using recycled material, plant-
   ing a tree, or donating to saving an animal on the endangered species
   list.

6) **MERMAID LORE**
   What is the history of the mermaid? What are some other nautical
   superstitions legends and myths? Contrast and compare them with
   theatre superstitions.

7) **BURY TREASURE!**
   Hold a treasure hunt as a fundraiser. Hide some prizes (tickets to the
   show? A poster autographed by the cast?) and draft a map and charge
   admission for a scavenger hunt!

www.ingramcontent.com/pod-product-compliance
Lightning Source LLC
Chambersburg PA
CBHW070421120726
47909CB00005B/1737